RANDY'S DANDY LIONS

written and illustrated by BILL PEET

HOUGHTON MIFFLIN COMPANY BOSTON

To my wife Margaret and my sons Bill and Steve

ISBN: 0-395-18507-6 REINFORCED EDITION
ISBN: 0-395-27498-2 SANDPIPER EDITION
PRINTED IN U.S.A.
Y 20 19 18 17 16 15 14 13 12 11

A fine lion tamer named Randy Monroe
Performed for a circus a long time ago
And the five big shaggy-maned lions of Randy's
Were billed in the show as the five fancy dandies.
But strangely enough very few people knew
What fantastic tricks the five lions could do
Because they were timid and suffered from cage fright
The same kind of fear that an actor calls stage fright.

When the circus began and the big top was packed
And they came out with Randy to put on their act,
The lions forgot about doing their stunts.
With a tent full of people all staring at once
They suddenly froze, couldn't budge from their places
With baffled and terrified looks on their faces
All except Dudley the bravest of all
Who had just enough courage to stand on a ball
So the act was a flop and the crowd became rude.
They all stamped their feet, while they hissed and they booed.

One night Colonel Bowers the circus's boss
Complained to poor Randy his act was a loss.
"What you need is a whip because once they get whacked
Those lions will soon put some life in their act."
"Oh, no," Randy pleaded, "I wouldn't dare beat them.
They're my very best friends, so I couldn't mistreat them."
"Well, we can't sell the lions," growled old Colonel Bowers.
"Used lions aren't worth much, especially ours.
We are stuck with these moth-eaten lions," he said,
"So we'll hire a new lion-tamer instead."

Poor Randy began his new job the next day
The biggest of all in the show, in a way.
He was handed a ladder along with a broom

And sent off to work as an elephant groom.
He swept all the dust off the elephants' hides
Behind their big ears, off their backs and both sides.

When the lions came into the big cage that night
They were stopped in their tracks by a horrible sight,
A powerful man with a fierce black mustache
Wearing a helmet and fiery red sash.
He was armed with a chair and a pistol and whip
A long snaky whip with a sting on the tip.

When he cracked his long whip, they were so terrified
That they frantically tried to find somewhere to hide
But hiding was useless the lions discovered.
Try as they might they left some part uncovered
And the cruel cracking whip lashed out through the air
Snapping off whiskers and large tufts of hair.

At last they just couldn't stand any more
And in desperation they started to roar,
Like a deep rolling rumble of thunder it went
Up from the ground to the top of the tent.

When they returned to their wagon that night
They were still so upset from their horrible fright,
That they couldn't stop roaring, they kept on and on
Long after the show when the people had gone.
"That's enough," cried the Colonel, "now you'd better be quiet!

Or I'll soon put you all on a head-lettuce diet!
And if that doesn't fix you then I'll tell you what,
I'll tie all your tails in a triple square knot!"
But the worst things the old Colonel threatened to do
Couldn't scare them one bit after what they'd been through.

"I know," said a clown, "what'll stop them I'll bet.
We'll douse them with water, lions hate to get wet.
Let's fill all the buckets and tubs we can find
Then call out the elephants. They'll make them mind."

Using their trunks just like fire hoses,
They aimed at the lions, right straight at their noses.
They drenched them until the poor beasts were half drowned
And for a few minutes there wasn't a sound.

Then they soon caught their breaths and started once more
To roar even louder than ever before.
"Let's all go to bed," grumbled old Colonel Bowers,
"They'll run out of roars in a couple of hours."

But as it so happened the Colonel was wrong
The lions continued to roar all night long
So loud and so deep that it made the ground shake
And kept everyone in the circus awake.

But they couldn't keep roaring forever, of course,
And little by little the lions grew hoarse.

At six in the morning they fell off to sleep
On the floor of their cage in a big tousled heap.

When the Colonel woke up it was already noon
And the one o'clock show must be set to go soon.
He couldn't get dressed, there was no time for that,
So he rushed from his tent in his nightshirt and hat.
"Wake up now!" he shouted. "On your feet everyone!
The show must go on! There's a lot to be done!"

Soon all the roustabouts swarmed from their tent
Yawning and rubbing their eyes as they went
In a hurry to make up the time they had lost
And get the show ready to go at all cost
But all the confusion and rushing about
Was entirely for nothing it finally turned out.

As the grand procession approached the big top,
The elephants suddenly came to a stop
They had fallen asleep right there in their tracks
Just as limp and as saggy as old gunny sacks.
They couldn't go on, and no one could make them,
Even the loud circus band couldn't wake them.

The camels were always bad tempered and rude
And a night without sleep hadn't helped their mean mood.
They wailed and they moaned and they loudly complained
Then sat down on their haunches and there they remained.
The zebras were mulish, they kicked up their heels
And knocked off their fancy gold chariot's wheels.

The poor clowns were just barely able to wake up
And put on their costumes, their noses and makeup
But they were too drowsy to hold up their heads
They finally gave up and flopped down on their beds.

It was useless to try and get things underway
So the Colonel decided to call it a day.
And he went in the big top to do some explaining
To the crowd which by this time had started complaining.
"I'm terribly sorry," he said with a yawn,
"We're all much too sleepy, the show can't go on.
I'll return all your money, yes, every last cent
If you'll meet me outside right in front of the tent."

However, before Colonel Bowers retired
He fired the new lion-tamer he'd hired
And the frightening fellow walked off in a huff
With his whip and his chair and the rest of his stuff.

Then he went to the lions and gave each a poke
With the end of his cane and they slowly awoke.
"Now look here," he said, "I am not a mean man

So I'll try to be just as fair as I can.
You'll get one more chance. If you fail to come through,
I'll haul every one of you off to the zoo!''

And that one more chance was all that they needed
For Randy's five lions at last had succeeded
In overcoming their case of cage fright
For nothing could frighten them after that night.
When they entered the cage you could tell by their faces
They were eager and ready to go through their paces.

First Buford went bouncing around in the ring
With his tail curled up under him just like a spring
And Sam rode a cycle with only one wheel
While he balanced a ball on his nose like a seal.
Dudley hung by his heels from a flying trapeze
Where he swung to and fro with the greatest of ease.

Dudley and Melvin teamed up in some stunts.
They leaped through a hoop, that is both at once.
This trick was most often a matter of luck
Two times out of three they ended up stuck
But the routine which called for the most skill was Milt's
He walked all about on a tall pair of stilts.

To top their performance the last thing they did
Was to balance themselves in a grand pyramid
So very precise and so very exact
That one slip of a paw could upset the whole act.
Or even a sneeze could cause them to fall
And then down came Randy, lions and all
But in spite of these mishaps, they caused a sensation
The crowd cheered them on with a rousing ovation.

When the circus was over they all went to sleep
With big smiles on their faces in one shaggy heap
For their fear of big crowds was a thing of the past.
Randy's five dandy lions were happy at last.